Last Day at Sharp Park

a fantasy novella

David R. Beshears

Adapted from the pilot episode
screenplay of the television series
"Miles Bennett"

Greybeard Publishing
Washington State

Greybeard Publishing
P.O. Box 480
McCleary, WA 98557-0480

ISBN 978-0-9987535-4-6
(large print edition)

Last Day at Sharp Park

Chapter One

The small, rundown motel had long ago been converted to four tiny, drab apartments. It sat at the end of a narrow road, the road ending at a small gravel lot in front of the motel. A man-made embankment separated the beach from the motel and the lot.

A grandmotherly woman in her late sixties stepped out of one of the apartments. She had a kind face encircled by short, wavy gray hair, wore a faded pattern dress. She walked across to a bench at the edge of the lot, the world about her enveloped in a slowly drifting fog.

The sound of a bus reached out from the fog. Just visible in the gray mist, the late-fifties school bus stopped at the intersection a hundred yards up the road where the road met the street. Half a minute later the bus departed and moments later the silhouette of a small boy formed in the fog as he walked down the road.

Anna stood and waited. Seeing his grandma, six year old Jack grinned and hurried to her.

He was a small boy and painfully thin. He had wild, blonde hair, was dressed in faded blue jeans, a button shirt and a light jacket.

They hugged briefly and then pulled apart.

"Hello, Jack," said Grandma. "And how was school today?"

Jack grinned. "You ask me that every day, Grandma. Every, every day."

"And I'll be standing right here tomorrow, and I'll ask you again."

They hugged again and then Anna took the boy by the hand.

"How about a walk on the beach before we go inside?"

Will Bennett started back up the long driveway from the wrought-iron double-gate toward the house. He had a bundle of mail in hand and was absently looking through it as he walked.

Will was in his mid-twenties, was slim without being thin. His thick hair curled around his ears. His pants and shirt were contemporary, casual, comfortable.

The grounds surrounding the large, two-storey house consisted of a sprawling lawn that could use a mowing, and a scattering of shrubs and trees. The house was a large, square structure with a covered front deck that spanned the width of the house from one corner to the other.

Will took his attention from the mail long enough to climb the steps up onto the covered porch and approach the large front door.

The foyer was a large, open room. There were doors to the left and right, and a staircase directly across from the front door.

Will closed the door behind him and started to the open door on the right. His sister Ellinor came into the foyer and followed Will toward the west wing hallway.

Ellinor Bennett was a year younger than her brother. She had wavy, shoulder-length brown hair, and was wearing comfortable slacks and blouse that showed her figure without really calling attention to it.

Will acknowledged her as they entered the hallway. It was wide, carpeted; several lamps were set high on the walls, spreading a golden glow.

"Sister."

"Brother," said Ellinor.

"How was your trip?" Will was again sorting through the mail. "You came in pretty late last night."

"Oh, Will… you'd have just loved it."

Will gave an absent grin to the sarcasm. "Sounds exciting."

"Thrilling."

Will gave one of the letters another look, handed it to Ellinor.

"Another one from Jason Anders," he said.

Ellinor glanced at the envelope without really looking at it. She handed it back.

"Grandfather's business."

"The second one in a week." Will's expression grew thoughtful. "I know I've heard that name before. Don't know where. *Anders.* Have you heard that name before?"

They reached an open double-door on their right and turned into the dining room. A large table occupied the center of the room. The wall behind the head of the table had a large window, and there was a fireplace in the center of the wall opposite the door.

Miles Bennett, the patriarch of the Bennett family, sat at the head of the table reading a newspaper. A glass of orange juice sat on the table in front of him.

Miles was well-dressed and well-groomed. He was in his sixties, had salt-and-pepper hair, and an air of calm, confident sophistication about him.

Will set the mail onto a side table and he followed Ellinor to a buffet that ran the length of the wall beside the doorway. On the buffet was a tray of breakfast rolls, a pitcher of orange juice and juice glasses, a covered dish of bacon, another of scrambled eggs.

"Good morning, Grandfather," said Ellinor, speaking over her shoulder. She began filling her plate.

"Good morning, Ellinor." Miles glanced up briefly, returned to his newspaper. "I trust your trip went well?"

"Well enough." She filled a glass with orange juice and started to the table. "The final paperwork from the attorney should arrive this afternoon. Work on the wind farm should start the beginning of the month."

Mrs. Bailey came into the room carrying a bowl of assorted cubed fruit. She stood beside Will and made room on the buffet for the bowl.

"Good morning, Mrs. Bailey," said Will. He eyed the fruit. "Don't ever leave me, Mrs. Bailey."

Mrs. Bailey was in her sixties, was a bit shorter than average, a bit heavier than average. She spoke with calm self-assuredness.

"Good morning, Master William. You really should see about getting a life." She turned about to look to Miles. "I'll be away this afternoon, Mr. Bennett. I'll set

out sandwich fixings for lunch before I
go."

"Thank you, Mrs. Bailey," said Miles.
"You are very kind."

Mrs. Bailey nodded and left the room
as Will carried his breakfast over to the
table and sat down beside his sister.

"I do love that woman," he said.

"Of course you do," said Ellinor.
"She's spoiled you rotten your whole
life."

"Not so." Will considered as he took a
bite of fruit. "She helped me with my
homework now and then."

"You spent your entire childhood in
her kitchen."

"Where she helped me with my
homework."

Mr. Gray entered the dining room
then, pausing briefly to take in the
scene. He was sixty years old, tall,
dressed in a dark suit. He had a calm,
steady demeanor about him.

"Ah, Mr. Gray." Miles folded his newspaper and set it aside. "Have you seen Alice yet this morning?"

"I believe she is in the study, Mr. Bennett," said Mr. Gray, taking a single step nearer Miles.

"Aunt Alice has been really moody lately," said Will, taking another bite of fruit. "I mean, from her normal level seven moody up to a ten."

"Yes, I have noticed the shift in her disposition as well." Miles took a drink of his juice. "We will give her time, and space, for now."

"Something's up," said Will.

"As I said," Miles sighed dismissively. He turned to Mr. Gray. "Apologies, Mr. Gray. You wished to speak with me?"

Mr. Gray gave a slight nod. "The confirmation request arrived regarding your attendance at the High Council meeting scheduled for this morning."

"I replied?" asked Miles. "Am I looking forward to the meeting?"

"You did. And of course you are."

"Of course I am. Thank you so much, Mr. Gray."

"Of course, sir." Mr. Gray stepped back, gave a nod of acknowledgement to the others at the table. "Master William, Mistress Ellinor." He started back to the door, noted the bundle of mail and stepped to the side table.

"William," he stated. "If you insist on collecting the mail, then I must insist that once you have finished sorting through it that you complete the delivery by bringing it to my office."

"Sure, Mr. Gray. Anything to help." Will took another bite of breakfast, looked then across to Miles. "Grandfather... you got another letter from Jason whoever. Second one this week."

Miles looked from Will over to Mr. Gray. "Mr. Gray?"

"I'll take care of it, sir." Mr. Gray left the dining room.

Miles looked to Will. "Mr. Gray will take care of it." He took another swallow of juice.

"Right. Sure…" Will grew introspective. "I know that name. *Anders*. Where have I heard that name? Is something up?"

"Nothing is up," stated Miles. "A personal matter. That's all."

"Right…" Will glanced over at the door through which Mr. Gray had departed. "Right… And Mr. Gray will take care of it."

The study was a room of warm woods, warmly glowing lamps, thick pile carpet, built-in book shelves and a fireplace inset into the long wall. Alice stood at the one window at the far end of the room. The drape was pulled aside enough for her to see outside, sunlight on her face.

Alice looked to be in her late forties, tall and thin. She was dressed in a long-sleeve blouse and full-length skirt. Her long brown hair was pulled back into a thick ponytail.

She didn't acknowledge Miles coming into the room, continuing to look out the window.

"Good morning, Alice," said Miles. He moved to his desk and settled into his leather chair. "We missed you at breakfast."

"Good morning, Father." Alice spoke without turning. "I'll get something later."

Miles pulled a stack of folders to him and opened one. He lifted out an open envelope with a letter stapled to it. He read it silently.

Alice held her arms across her chest, cupping her elbows in her palms. She gave a side-glance to Miles as he put the letter back into the folder.

"From Jason?" she asked absently.

"Nothing of any importance." He set the folder aside and opened the next one in the stack.

Alice grew thoughtful, continued to look out the window, to let the sunlight wash over her face.

"How is your project coming?"

"Quite well," said Miles. "Thank you."

"Wind farm. Interesting."

"I think so." Miles picked up a pen and began making notes in the margins of an official looking document.

"And most philanthropic," said Alice.

"I suppose that's so. It should provide enough electricity to support the entire town."

The town, a mile and a half down the road, had a population of just over 30,000.

"Which you will provide at cost." Alice now did turn to look at her father. "And you intend to offer the land on which the wind farm will sit to local the farmers at no cost."

"Our contribution to the cause, my dear."

Alice turned back to the window. "The Society isn't going to like it."

"Not their concern."

"Of course it is. And you know it."

"I don't answer to them."

"You <u>are</u> them."

Miles leaned back in his chair, rolled his pen through his fingers. He said nothing.

"Your philanthropy is generating publicity," said Alice. "That makes you visible. And that makes the Society nervous."

Miles turned slowly about in his chair and gave Alice a studied look.

"That is not what is bothering you. Is it?"

Alice hesitated, finally acknowledged the question. "No, Father. We can deal with the Society."

"You more than I, I should think," said Miles. "And so?"

Alice continued to stare thoughtfully out the window. She took in a long breath, let it out slow. She held a hand up before her, her palm to the sunlight.

"A shadow passed before my eyes," she said. "Three days ago. I reached out to it, but I hesitated… I'm sorry."

"The shadow. Light or dark?"

"I don't know." Alice let her hand drift nearer the window, held it up near the pane of glass without quite touching it. "It remains near, just beyond my sight. It is drawn here. It is… searching; that, and something more. There is sadness."

"Can you tell—"

"If I knew more…" said Alice, cutting him off. She turned her head slowly from the window, looked to her father. "The boy is nearby?"

Miles didn't answer at first. He looked up at his daughter, then away.

"Not far," he said softly. "Is it related, then?"

"You can reach him." It was a statement more than a question.

"If need be."

Alice turned again to the window, her face to the sun. "Perhaps you should do that."

"Meeting," grumbled Miles. "Later, perhaps."

The windowless room was lined with bookshelves. A round table sat in the center of the room, with three chairs evenly spaced around the table. An opening in one wall revealed the study beyond.

Miles brought a wooden box down from a shelf and set it on the table. The box was nine inches square, made of fine wood and set with small brass latches and hinges.

He lifted a latch on the box, lifted the lid, and lowered the lid and one attached side onto the tabletop. This revealed a crystal cube within the box. The cube was eight inches square.

He lowered the remaining sides of the box. He reached out, rested a hand on the top of the cube. It began to pulsate.

He sat back in his chair, continuing to focus on the cube. The pulsating stopped, the glow brightened, and in moments filled the room.

Miles was sitting at the same table, only now he was in the Council Chamber. The room beyond the table was hidden in darkness.

The other two chairs were occupied.

One council member was a gray haired woman in her sixties, dressed in a heavy, multi-colored robe with a high collar.

The other council member, also in his sixties, was a tall man with salt-and-pepper hair and a well-trimmed beard. He wore a tan, collarless jacket.

"Good morning, Miles," said the councilwoman.

Miles nodded to her, then to the councilman.

"Good morning," he said.

"Shall we get the meeting started?" asked the councilwoman. She brought her hands together, steepled her fingers. "Miles. I understand we may have issue with Jason Anders."

Chapter Two

Ellinor turned into a narrow hallway, followed it to an open door on the right and entered Mr. Gray's office. It was a mirror image to her grandfather's study. Bookshelves lined the wall opposite the door, and to Ellinor's left a single window in the wall behind Mr. Gray's desk let in natural light.

"Mr. Gray," said Ellinor. "Have you seen Grandfather?"

"Council meeting, Miss Ellinor," said Mr. Gray. He looked up from his work and indicated the shelves along the wall.

Ellinor acknowledged that with a short nod, then looked restlessly about Mr. Gray's office. She glanced to the bookshelves, back finally to Mr. Gray.

"Has he been in there long?"

"I don't imagine he'll be much longer."

Ellinor hesitated, finally approached the wall. "Maybe I'll wait inside," she said at last.

Mr. Gray was again focused on his work. "As you wish, Miss Ellinor."

"I'll see you at lunch."

"Sandwiches," stated Mr. Gray, with very little enthusiasm.

Ellinor reached into the shelves and released a hidden catch. There was a solid clicking sound and a section of the shelf wall opened a few inches.

"I like sandwiches." She took a step back, pulled the shelf wall fully open, and entered the Closet.

The glow of the cube in the center of the table was just beginning to fade. Miles was sitting before it, his expression distant. The back wall behind him was slightly open, revealing his study beyond.

Ellinor watched and waited as the last of the glow of the cube began to dissipate. It was another fifteen or twenty seconds before Miles' focus returned fully to his surroundings.

He looked up at his granddaughter.

"Good morning, Ellinor." He began closing the box, lifting the sides and latching them into place. "What can I do for you?"

"How is the council taking the project?"

"The matter never came up." Miles finished closing box, slid it across to Ellinor. She took it and carried it over to the shelf.

"Something more important than the bright light of unwelcome publicity shining on the Society?" She slid the box into position on the shelf. "Is there something we should know?"

The thought crossed her mind that she sounded way too much like her brother.

Miles slid his chair back and stood up. "Nothing of interest, Granddaughter."

He started toward the opening to his study, Ellinor followed. Behind them, Mr. Gray closed the opening to his own office.

Entering the study, Miles walked over to his desk as Ellinor closed the access to the Closet.

She wasn't ready to let Grandfather's last comment go.

"You are being rather less than forthright, Grandfather," she stated coolly and took the two steps to stand before his desk.

"Sorry, my dear. Way of the world." Miles settled into his chair. "Is there something else I can help you with?"

Ellinor gave her grandfather as sharp look. She folded her arms across her chest.

"Jason Anders."

"What about him?"

"I did a little digging."

"Did you?"

"He's Society," she said. "It seems there was a big fuss-up about fifty years ago, which the Society managed to keep quiet."

Miles leaned back in his chair, looked up at Ellinor, seeming to consider a response.

"For the most part," he said at last. "Why the interest?"

"Will asked if the name sounded familiar. It did."

"I see… and so?"

"And so apparently his son went missing; disappeared with the boy's grandmother. Word at the time was that it had something to do with Jason."

"Such was the rumor," Miles said guardedly.

"And I could find nothing after that. Not a word. No one ever saw Grandma or the boy again."

"That's right."

"Now Jason Anders begins sending you letters; fresh one every couple of days. After all these years?"

Miles straightened in his chair, leaned over his desk, appeared ready to end the conversation.

"We were friends once. He's reaching out. Nothing more."

"Grandfather."

"There is nothing there that concerns you."

"Grandfather..." increasingly frustrated.

"I want you to let it go."

Ellinor held her silence. Her expression grew stern, her folded arms squeezed a little tighter. She stared intently at her grandfather.

The conversation was definitely at an end.

§

The old-style kitchen was high-ceilinged, airy, with lots of tall cabinets and plenty of counter space. It had been around for a long time, and yet was both efficient and comfortable.

Will sat at the large island counter, a glass of iced tea in hand as he watched Mrs. Bailey go about preparing trays of sandwich fixings.

"I'm telling you, Mrs. B, there's something going on in this house. Folks are acting real peculiar."

"I've been with your grandfather twice as long as you've been alive. I watched your father take his first steps, right there in your grandfather's study." Mrs. Bailey spoke as she continued about her work. "I don't recall a day gone by that there wasn't something peculiar going on in this house."

"I get that, but this is different. And it's not just Alice." Will considered that a moment. "Though I suppose her weirding way could have the others spooked."

"Your aunt's *weirding way* is a great gift," said Mrs. Bailey, managing a patient grin. "It has helped your grandfather more times than I can remember. Got your father out of a fix a time or two as well."

Will thought about that, looking down at his glass of iced tea. He took a drink, gently set the glass down on the table.

"I've always thought it strange that my father wasn't born with the same gift as Alice."

"Being twins doesn't make 'em the same. Your father has made do just fine with what he was given."

Will prepared to take another drink and then didn't. "Suppose so. And that would be more than me."

"Oh, poor William," said Mrs. Bailey. "Ya' got your wits, boy. And I expect there's a little of your family in you. You'll find it."

Will held his hand before him, rubbed his fingertips together. There was a faint sparking, each the size of a sand granule. He sighed, then looked fondly at Mrs. Bailey.

"Hey, I got you, Mrs. B. I'll make do with that."

"Uh, huh…" She pushed one of the trays across the counter. "Here. Take this into the dining room."

Ellinor came into the dining room, looked curiously about and then stepped over to the buffet. She spoke over her shoulder to Will as she began putting together a sandwich.

"Where is everyone?" she asked.

Will was sitting at the table munching on half a sandwich. The other half was on a plate in front of him beside a glass of milk.

"Here and gone." Will took another bite of his lunch. "Where you been?"

"Following up on a few things." She brought her lunch over to the table and sat down. "I think you were right about that Jason Anders."

She took a bite of her sandwich.

Miles entered the Closet, closed the opening leading from the study. He lifted the wooden box from its place on the shelf and set it on the table. He lifted a latch on the box, lifted the lid, lowered the top and one side onto the tabletop, revealing the crystal cube within the box.

Miles sat down then and lowered the remaining sides of the box. With the cube fully exposed, he rested two fingers on the cube. It began to pulsate.

§

Anna was standing on the beach watching the surf, the hint of melancholy on her face. Fog drifted across the beach. Miles approached through the mist. Anna didn't look at the approaching figure, neither did she appear to be surprised at the arrival.

Miles reached Anna and stood beside her. They stood together, looking out across the ocean.

"Anna," said Miles at last.

Will came into the study, Ellinor entering behind him.

There was no one there.

"Well, this is where he was headed," said Will. "He seemed a bit anxious about it, actually."

"That doesn't sound like Grandfather," said Ellinor. She nodded to the Closet access panel in the book shelf wall. "The Closet?"

Will gave a shrug and they stepped up to the shelves. Ellinor reached in and released the catch. There was the familiar solid click sound, and she pulled the access open.

The Closet was empty but for the cube on the table.

Will looked down at the cube. "He's in there?"

"Where else?" Ellinor stepped around to the side of the table.

"But they already had their Council meeting. I'm telling ya. Something is going on…"

"I brought up that very question."

"And?"

"You know Grandfather."

Will frowned at the cube. "Miles does have his secrets."

Alice came into the Closet then. Will and Ellinor watched her approach the table, watched as she looked thoughtfully down at the cube.

"Your grandfather has not gone to the Council Chamber," she said.

"I don't understand," said Will. "Where else would he be?"

"The Nexus Cube is addressing somewhere else." Alice lifted a hand, held it palm out midway to the glowing cube.

"I knew it," Ellinor whispered heavily.

"I didn't know it could do that," said Will. "I thought it was just the door to the Chamber."

"Of course it can do that," said Ellinor. She looked to Alice. "Where is he? Where did he go? To Jason?"

"Not to Jason," said Alice. "Sharp Park. The boy."

Ellinor took a moment to catch her breath. "Can we go there?" she asked then.

Will looked uncertain. "Ell?"

Alice looked to Will, then to Ellinor. She indicated the chairs.

"Sit."

She waited for them to sit down, then reached out, lightly rested two fingers on the cube.

An elderly woman's bedroom, gray and dull; a small bed, an old, four-drawer dresser upon which sat a cheap jewelry box with a miniature plastic ballerina on the lid.

Will and Ellinor entered the room from the small closet, pushing their way through half a dozen old, faded dresses. Ellinor moved cautiously into the middle of the room, looking about for signs of danger. Will stood just outside the closet.

"That was rather stale," he mumbled, brushing dust off his shirt.

"I don't think we're in Kansas, Toto."

"I don't think we're in the twenty first century, Dorothy." Will studied the room. "Nineteen sixties, I'd say."

They left the bedroom and went into the living room. There was a couch and an easy chair, a black and white console television; a dinette set in the kitchen area; all a snapshot out of the early 60s.

No one home.

"Curiouser and curiouser," said Will. "Definitely early sixties."

Ellinor poked her head into the other bedroom. It was just large enough for a twin bed and a dresser; plain, no decorations. Atop the dresser was a small collection of plastic toys; toy soldiers, cars.

She stepped back into the middle of the living room.

"I don't think Grandfather was expecting to deal with this today. This surprised him."

"That may be. Either way, Miles knows a lot more than he's telling."

"That's my point," said Ellinor. "He's not telling anything."

That is so Miles… thought Will.

"Well, according to Alice, he's here. Somewhere."

"Wherever here is," said Ellinor.

"*Whenever* here is."

Ellinor gave a nod to the front door. Will gave a short nod in answer.

They came out of the apartment and onto the front stoop. They hesitated a moment at the sheer bleakness of it all, then stepped out into the narrow road.

There was a gravel parking to their right, where road ended. A short embankment ran beside the motel and parking lot. The sound of gentle surf reached them from the other side of the embankment. To their left, the road disappeared into the fog.

The entire world was ugly and run down.

"Do you suppose it's always this miserable?" asked Will. "Or are we here on a particularly bad day?"

They both turned about and looked behind them at the building they had come out of.

"Roach motel?" Ellinor wondered aloud.

"Converted to apartments." Will looked carefully at the handful of small windows and narrow doors. "Most of 'em look empty."

They turned about again. Ellinor made a face.

"Do you smell that?"

"Rotting seaweed." Will indicated a set of grayed wooden steps that ran up the short embankment. "Shall we?"

"If we have to." Ellinor started toward the steps. "Not your typical tourist destination."

Chapter Three

Miles and Anna were walking casually along the beach. The tide had retreated some and the sand beneath their feet was damp but firm. The fog had thinned a little, though the sky overhead remained gray.

"How's the boy?" asked Miles.

"He's doing well. You know Jack." They walked in silence for a few moments, each lost in their own thoughts. "And so, your visit... has Jason found us?"

"Possibly. I don't know. Not yet."

They stopped walking. Anna looked side-glance at Miles.

"You don't know?" she asked.

"It was Alice." Miles shrugged. "Very cryptic."

Anna looked curiously, piercingly at Miles. He shook his head dismissively.

"Yes," he said. "Typically Alice."

A movement caught his attention. He turned his head and looked up the beach. Ellinor and Will were standing atop the embankment at the parking lot.

Miles grimaced, obviously not pleased at seeing them.

"Anna, I do apologize."

"Quite all right. They belong to you?"

"The grandchildren."

"Oh my," said Anna. "The last I recall, they were just babies. Now look at them."

Miles smirked. "They really haven't changed that much."

The statement drifted into silence. Miles looked tiredly at his grandchildren in the distance. Anna watched him, waited. She finally raised a brow, silently urging Miles forward.

"Very well," he stated. They started up the beach. Reaching the embankment, they climbed up to stand with Ellinor and Will.

"Hello, Grandfather," said Ellinor. "Would you mind explaining this?"

"I would mind. Very much. You need to leave."

"I don't think we can do that, sir," said Will.

Miles sighed heavily and turned to Anna. "Again, I am so sorry."

"Not at all, Clive," said Anna.

At hearing the name Clive, Will and Ellinor looked curiously at Miles, but said nothing for the moment.

Anna reached out to shake hands with the young people.

"Gregory and Donna's children, I understand."

"That's right," said Ellinor, warily. She looked side-glance at Miles.

"So nice to meet you," said Anna. She turned to Miles. "You must excuse me, Clive. I have to see to Jack. He'll be coming home soon."

"Of course." Miles watched Anna take the steps down to the parking lot.

"*Clive*, Miles?" asked Will.

"At one time."

The words were cool, distant. Will and Ellinor waited for something more. Nothing more came. Below, Anna crossed the gravel lot and stood beside the bench.

"You know her," stated Will.

"This is none of your concern."

"Of course it is."

"We're family, Grandfather," said Ellinor. "Don't push us away."

The school bus arrived then, stopping at the end of the road. The little boy Jack walked out of the fog and approached his grandma.

"What's going on, Grandfather?" asked Ellinor.

"I should think that was obvious. Jack is coming home from school."

"You know what I mean," Ellinor said, a forced calm. "The woman, the boy…

They haven't aged a day in fifty years. Have they?"

Miles ignored her, ignored the question. He quietly watched Jack and his grandma go through their daily ritual.

Ellinor pushed on. "It's more than just magic. Isn't it? It's this place."

Miles continued to ignore her, to ignore them both, his attention focused on the scene below them, the far side of the parking lot.

"That boy does adore his grandma," Will said absently.

Miles started down the steps.

"We're leaving."

A shadowed room with book-lined walls, a large desk in the center. The view beyond the window revealed a dark night.

The heavy door opened and Carlson, a tall, thin, very proper gentleman in his

mid-sixties, entered Jason Anders'
library. The butler stood to one side and
Jason followed Carlson into the room.

Jason was in his seventies, appeared
withered and as faded as the house
coat he wore. His gray hair was wispy
and near white.

He walked toward the desk as
Carlson went to a cabinet set against
the far wall. The butler brought back a
small, ornate chest, set it carefully on
the desk. Jason waved him dismissively
aside with one hand and stepped up
before the desk.

"Will there be anything else, Mr.
Anders?" asked Carlson.

"Nothing, nothing," grumbled Jason.
"Go away."

Carlson gave a barely perceptible
nod as he took a step back. He turned
and started toward the door. Jason
peered up through his bushy eyebrows
at the closing door. Only then did he
reach into the pocket of his house coat

and take out a key. He inserted it into the chest's lock, turned it. It gave a satisfying click. Jason lifted the lid.

He reached into the chest and brought out a cloth-covered package, set it on the desktop beside the chest. He carefully unfolded the cloth, exposing a hundred year old book. He brushed a wrinkled hand over the cover.

The book visibly trembled.

Jason carefully opened the book, slid a hand delicately across the pages. The book trembled again, the pages fluttered. The sound was dry and crisp.

Jason slowly sat, gave a thin smile. He laid his hand again on the book.

Now… my dear boy…

Miles was alone in his study. It was late, the house was quiet. He was sitting in one of the easy chairs, reading by the

light of the pole lamp standing beside
the chair.

A muffled shuffling sound disturbed
the quiet. Miles glanced up, looked
curiously about.

There was no movement. The silence
returned.

Miles returned to his book.

The shuffling sound again...

Miles looked up again. He glanced
then to the bookshelves. He leaned
forward.

An old book, leather spine, sat alone
on the shelf just at eye level.

Miles stood, eyes not leaving the
book.

The book appeared to shudder, if
only slightly; a hollow, shuffling sound.

Miles walked over to the shelf. He
reached out haltingly, grasped the book.
He carried it over to the desk, set it on
the desktop. He held his hand out over
the book, delicately brushed two fingers

across the leather cover. It vibrated at his touch.

He brushed his fingers across the book again.

The book opened on its own. A moment passed and all was still, quiet. A page rose then, turned. The turn of another page, and then another.

The book grew still. A thin wisp of fog rose up, lingered just above the book. There were silhouettes in the fog; movement… people.

Miles stared uneasily at the book, the fog, the silhouettes… a woman and a small boy.

Jason… what are you up to?

Jason lifted is hand from the pages of the leather-bound book, his fingers raised and slightly apart. A thin wisp of misty fog followed the hand's movement. Within the fog, the ethereal image of Jack, of Anna; of the beach.

Jason gave a gentle, sympathetic smile.

Warm morning light streamed into the dining room. Miles sat at the head of the table, his newspaper folded and sitting on the table beside his cup of coffee and a small dish with an untouched breakfast roll.

Alice stood at the window, the warmth of the early sun on her face. Will was at the buffet preparing a plate of scrambled eggs, bacon, and fruit. Ellinor was sitting at the table, holding a cup of coffee in both hands.

Miles moved his cup and dish aside, looked to Will at the buffet, then to Ellinor.

"I believe Jason has found them," he stated flatly.

"Excuse me?" asked Ellinor.

"Jason Anders. He has found them."

"I see."

Will moved from the buffet to the table.

"Actually, I could use a bit more info."

Miles gave an absent nod, gathering his thoughts as he watched Will take the chair next to his sister.

"As you have no doubt surmised, Jason was a wizard; is a wizard; a wizard with… passable talents. Nothing extraordinary, but passable. He has long been dissatisfied with his less than extraordinary abilities and so has continually strived to improve upon them."

"I would call that a positive personality trait," said Will, munching on a piece of fruit.

"Yes, well… that depends very much on the personality involved." Miles rested his elbows on the table, clasped his hands. "And he was also burdened

with being a sorcerer out of his time.
Specifically, the mid-twentieth century. A
particularly awkward era in which to be
a wizard of mediocre abilities. One was
plagued with being looked upon as a
sideshow magician of top hats and
bunny rabbits."

"No one believed in wizards
anymore," Alice said matter-of-factly.
She spoke softly, her face aglow in the
sunlight. "All to the good so far as the
Society was concerned. It allowed us to
once again retreat into the shadows."

Miles acknowledged the comment
with a nod, then continued.

"And then there was Jack. His son.
The boy was showing signs of
exceptional conjurer power even before
he could walk. This drove Jason nearly
mad. Not that he had far to go.
Obsessed with his desire to grow
beyond his limited talents, nothing he
did helped. He managed to acquire a
few artifacts, became moderately

successful in business, but nothing made him a better wizard."

"Or a better person," suggested Ellinor.

"Yes. Exactly," said Miles. "Meanwhile, Jack's abilities grew stronger. Untrained in the budding mind of a six year old boy, it became impossible to hide his talents from the real world. Anna grew fearful of what Jason might do to Jack to acquire the boy's abilities."

"So Grandma took the boy," said Will. He stabbed a piece of fruit with his fork.

"And they went into hiding," said Miles, nodding.

"For half a century?" asked Ellinor.

"And why there?" asked Will.

Alice continued her focus to the morning sun beyond the window. She closed her eyes, let the sun's rays feed her.

"The beach is here," she stated. The room grew quiet. Miles stared ahead, to some empty spot across the table.

Will looked up from his plate over to Alice.

"Here? Alice?"

"It's here," she said, hardly above the whisper. "They are here. At the estate."

Alice looked from the window to Miles, who continued to look across the table, his hands clasped in front of him.

"That place," she continued. "It is hidden by very powerful magic."

"You're hiding them?" Will asked Miles.

"No. I am not hiding them." Miles pulled his hands back, turned and looked at Alice. She looked directly at him, her gaze betraying no emotion. She said nothing.

Miles looked again to Will and Ellinor.

"The boy. Soon after they arrived, he removed it from the physical realm." He frowned, pursed his lips. "It is real. It does exist. It just isn't... physical."

"It's not physical..." Will sounded dubious. "It's not physical, but it's here."

Ellinor curled her brow, staring down at her coffee cup. Her expression suggested that she was starting to get it.

"Not just the passage, but that world. Is here."

"Exactly. Well, sort of." Miles looked pointedly at those in the room. "The important thing now is that I believe Jason has found them."

Miles stepped off the front stoop of Anna's apartment and walked toward the bench at the edge of the gravel lot. He reached it just as Anna and Jack came over the top of the embankment from the beach and started down the wooden steps.

Miles gave them a warm smile as they walked across the lot.

"Good evening, Clive," said Anna.

"Anna." Miles looked to the boy. "Hello, Jack."

Jack gave only a slight smile, the barest hint of a nod. Miles looked again to Anna and indicated the bench.

"Do you have a minute?" he asked. "We need to talk."

"Of course." Anna moved around the bench, an arm around Jack's shoulders.

Miles waited for them to sit down, then sat down beside them.

Alice came out of the study and started down the hall, on her way upstairs. She was half lost in thought when Mr. Gray came up behind her, walked beside her. They spoke as they walked.

"Miss Bennett."

"Yes, Mr. Gray?"

"Your brother called earlier. He wishes to speak with you. At your convenience."

"Thank you, Mr. Gray," she said. "I'll be in my room."

"Yes, Ma'am." Mr. Gray slowed, turned back as Alice continued.

Entering the foyer, Alice took the main stairs up to the second floor hall and on to her rooms.

The front sitting room of her suite was informal and open. There were assorted comfortable chairs, floor lamps and side tables. Her bedroom and bath were through a set of sliding double doors.

She walked around behind her desk, the wall behind her covered with full drapes. The drapes were open and revealed a large window, allowing sunlight to stream through.

As she moved between desk and window, the computer monitor turned on. Looking out the window, she casually lifted her hand and raised two fingers. The monitor flickered with images, the screen filled with a nature scene. She folded her arms and waited.

An image of a man's face appeared on the screen.

Gregory Bennett looked very much like Alice, his twin sister, though at the moment his hair was a bit wild and he could use a shave.

"Hello, sister," he said.

"Hello, Gregory." Alice looked briefly back at the screen, turned again to the window. "I understand you need to speak with me."

"I'm doing fine, Alice. Thanks for asking. Yourself?"

"Sorry," she said softly. "You are worried about me, yes?"

"As a matter of fact… you have been troubled these past few days."

"And you reach out halfway around the world because you sense my moodiness…"

"You know it's more than that, Alice. You are concerned. I too sense the shadow near you."

"Yes," she said. "It is near."

Gregory grew reflective, thoughtful. "I do not feel it as deeply as you, but it is strong."

Alice now turned away from the window, looked directly at the monitor. She continued to clasp her arms about her.

"I believe it has something to do with the boy."

"The boy?" asked Gregory. He thought a moment. "Jack? After all this time? All these years?"

"I am almost certain."

Gregory grew quiet for several moments. Alice waited.

"Perhaps," he said at last. "Perhaps, yes. And yet, there is… something else."

"Perhaps that is what is troubling me. It is as yet so unclear." Alice looked away from the image of her brother. "So, brother. How are things with you? The Andes treating you well?"

"The Andes are beautiful, if somewhat lacking in oxygen."

"And Donna?"

Gregory looked briefly off camera, back to Alice.

"Beautiful, if somewhat lacking in oxygen."

There was a long pause, then. Gregory's expression grew solemn.

"Go to the boy," he said.

Alice again looked briefly at the monitor, again out the window.

"See you soon, brother."

"The Gathering. Three weeks. Don't be late."

"I'll be there."

Alice raised two fingers, her arms still folded across her chest. The monitor grew dark.

She fully faced the window then. She closed her eyes, her head drifted back, relaxed. The light and the warmth of the sun washed over her face, warmed her, fed her.

Chapter Four

Will was sitting on the bench at the edge of the parking lot, looking patiently up the road, into the fog. Ellinor came out of the apartment, started across to her brother.

"No one here," he said.

Ellinor sat down beside her brother, followed his gaze up the road.

"This place is always the same," she said.

"Dreary."

"No. I mean the same. Literally the same. It never changes."

The sound of the school bus then, approaching and coming to a stop at the end of the road, half-hidden in the fog. It left a few moments later, leaving behind only silence.

Will and Ellinor waited… but there
was no little boy.

"Well, that's interesting," said Ellinor.
She looked questioning at Will.

"Curiouser and curiouser," said Will.
"What was that about change?"

Ellinor leaned forward, slowly stood
up. She turned about and looked across
the parking lot to the embankment.

"What say we look around?"

Will agreed silently. They walked
across the small lot and took the steps
up to the top of the embankment. The
fog had begun to thin somewhat and
they were able to see a short distance
up the beach. Alice was standing near
the surf's edge.

"Now that's really curious," said Will.
"Alice outside the estate?"

"This is the estate. Remember?"

"Right. No," droned Will doubtfully.
He looked up into the gray sky, again
toward Alice half-hidden in drifting

fog. "Not the best locale for the Sun Princess."

Ellinor frowned at her brother, started down the embankment to the beach.

"Come on."

They scrambled down the embankment and walked over to their aunt.

"Alice?" asked Ellinor. "What are you doing here?"

Alice did not respond at first. She looked out across the waves for a long time.

"Something's not right," she finally said, continuing to look out at the ocean.

"So we've noticed," said Will. He looked up and down the beach. The fog had begun to close in again, to thicken and darken. "Have you seen anyone else around?"

Alice looked away from the ocean, to Ellinor and to Will. She indicated then a set of footprints in the sand. The gentle, foamy surf reached the prints and was threatening to wash them away.

Ellinor looked down at the footprints, then up the beach in the direction the prints led.

"They look like Anna's," she said.

"Right," said Will. "Grandma."

"Made sometime after the last high tide." Ellinor started up the beach then without saying another word, following the tracks into the fog.

Will looked from Ellinor to Alice.

"Alice? You coming?"

The three of them worked their way up the beach, the fog drifting about them in a slight breeze.

"She walked alone," Will noted after half a minute or so.

"She went looking for the boy," said Ellinor.

"On the beach?"

"He wasn't on the bus."

"True." Will glanced curiously at Alice, who had again grown silent, then again to his sister. "The kid doesn't strike me as the kind to play hooky. So where do you think Grandma is headed?"

Ellinor indicated the top of the cliff that began to show itself, a wall of dark shadow materializing in the fog. It rose from the sands of the beach, eighty feet high, sloping back just slightly. A narrow, steep trail wound its way up to the top.

Will didn't like where this was going.

"You expect us to climb that? There's gotta be a way around."

"Anna did it."

Fine time for Alice to speak up.

"Yet to be determined, Aunt Alice."

"Come on, Will," said Ellinor. "Do you really want to wait down here while we're up there discovering the secrets of the universe?"

"Sure."

"Don't be a wuss." Ellinor stepped up to the foot of the cliff and started up the steep trail. Alice started forward then, glancing back to Will.

"William?"

"All right, all right." Will frowned darkly as he followed. "Why not? Let's find the hardest way to do everything, shall we?"

Jason stood at the front door of the Bennett house, glanced up and down the large deck as he waited. The door opened, revealing Miles.

Neither spoke at first, and Miles stepped outside.

"Jason." Miles eased the door closed behind him. "While I'm not surprised to see you, I must admit that I am rather surprised to see you *here*."

"Hello, Clive. You left me little choice."

"Did I?"

"It is important that I speak with you."

"Apparently." Miles hesitated, then indicated that they should walk. "Very well."

They moved to the steps and took them down to the concrete walk. Miles then led Jason off the walk and they started across the lawn.

Miles gave Jason a *talk to me* look...

"I need you to allow me in," said Jason.

They walked in silence for a few moments.

"I'm not the one preventing it," said Miles. They stopped, turned to face one another.

"Clive..."

"It's Miles, now."

"Really?" Jason frowned. "I assumed that was just for the public."

"No."

"Too bad."

"What do you want, Jason?"

"You did read my letters?"

"Mr. Gray responded, did he not?"

Jason studied Miles a moment. They started walking again.

"I have accepted my limitations, Miles. It didn't come easy, mind you, but I have." Jason thought carefully about his next words. "And my mortality, as well."

"Good," Miles stated flatly.

Jason looked almost deferentially at Miles. "Not an easy thing for we mortals to come to terms with."

"Jason…"

"No, I'm all right with it, now. Really. It's all right. It really is."

"I'm glad to hear it, Jason. I truly am. But I—"

"I have been looking for Mother and the boy. I want to tell them…" Jason's tone grew soft and melancholy. "I want to apologize; to the boy, to Mother. I want to tell them how sorry I am. Before I… well…"

They reached the corner of the house, started around to the side yard.

"I don't know if that will be possible, Jason."

Jason had no response to that. They continued to walk about the grounds, across the side yard.

"I'll see what I can do," said Miles.

The small, west-coast elementary school was right out of the early nineteen sixties. One wing of the building contained the classrooms, another the administration offices and library; the third wing was the cafeteria and gymnasium. The building sat in the center of a large, flat lot of asphalt, tufts of weed growing through the cracks. To one side was a playground of four-square, tetherball and dodge ball courts. There was an empty parking lot in front of the administration wing.

There was no one about.

Ellinor, Will and Aunt Alice started across the playground. They approached the apex of the building complex. A colorful poster on the wall of the building pictured a cartoon of the stop-drop-cover scenario, with a bright mushroom cloud rising in the background.

"*This do be* a school from the middle of the last century," said Will. "Back then, it was all about earthquakes and atom bombs."

"Scaring the hell out of little kids?" asked Ellinor.

"*Thems was the times*, Sister. Early sixties on the west coast."

They continued to a door and entered the building.

The central hallway of the classroom wing was wide, with glossy linoleum floors. Doors with inset narrow windows lined both sides of the empty hallway. The school was eerily quiet.

Ellinor and Will looked into several empty classrooms. Alice stopped at a drinking fountain that was set low for elementary school children. The fountain worked. She took a drink, wiped her mouth dry as she moved to a bulletin board on the wall beside the fountain. She silently read several of the posted notices.

"There's an assembly this Friday," she said dolefully.

Will turned from a classroom door to Alice.

"Attendance mandatory? That could be a problem."

Further down the hall, Ellinor stood at another door.

"Here," she called out softly.

She opened the door and went in as the others approached. Rows of first-grade desks faced the front of the class. A blackboard behind the teacher's desk spanned the front of the room. The wall opposite the door was filled with windows looking out onto the asphalt playground.

Jack was sitting at a desk in the middle of the otherwise empty classroom. He was looking forward, saying nothing, doing nothing.

"What's he doing?" whispered Will.

"What does it look like?" Ellinor shrugged a shoulder. "He's sitting in class."

Will studied the boy for a few moments more, then stepped around his sister and walked slowly over to stand beside the boy. The boy ignored him.

Will looked down at the desk in the next row directly beside the boy. He struggled then, managed with some difficulty to wiggle into it. He placed his hands on the desktop, clasped his fingers… and stared ahead, as the boy was doing.

Over by the door, Alice moved around to stand beside Ellinor. Her gaze was curious, almost penetrating. She tilted her head slightly to one side, studied the boy.

Nothing happened for a long time. Then Jack looked side-glance at Will, quickly forward again; a second time then, as quickly, covertly.

"Makes sense," said Ellinor. "Will is bound to connect with a six year old who's been around for half a century."

Ellinor and Alice were out in the hall, just outside the classroom. They had left Will with Jack a few minutes earlier, hoping the private time would give him more opportunity to connect with the boy.

"He does this every day..." Ellinor wondered aloud, looked over at Alice. "Jack."

"He comes here every day. As for what he does once he's here..." Alice shook her head. "Today is different."

"Today he didn't come home," agreed Ellinor. She looked through the narrow window in the door, into the classroom. "Will is talking to him… he's talking back." She looked away, contemplative. "The boy sits alone in an empty classroom. Is that—"

"We don't know that," said Alice, cutting her off. She responded then to Ellinor's curious look. "We don't know that it's empty."

"Um…"

"It's empty to us. Who knows what the boy sees? It may not be empty at all. To him."

"Wow," said Ellinor. "That's heavy."

There was a sound then from down the hall. Footsteps… Miles and Anna, approaching.

"I see you found her," Ellinor said to Miles, while looking at Anna.

"She was never lost."

"So, where have you been?"

"Teacher's lounge," Miles said, matter-of-factly. "Where else?"

The sound of the school bell rang throughout the halls and classrooms, faded then, leaving a hollow silence behind.

"Ah," said Miles. "There we go."

"Where we go?" asked Ellinor.

Alice's gaze drifted down the hall. She spoke in a distant whisper.

"Do you hear that?"

The hallway was quiet.

"Alice?" asked Ellinor.

The classroom door beside them opened, Will and Jack came out. Seeing Grandma, Jack appeared puzzled at first, but quickly broke into a broad smile.

"Grandma?" He hurried to her and they hugged. "Grandma!"

"Hello, dear." Anna brushed at the boy's hair with one hand. "Are you ready to go home?"

"Yep," said Jack. "Home?"

"Home, sweetie."

They turned and started down the hall, Miles walking beside them. Will gave a shrug and they all followed after them.

Alice stopped at the drinking fountain and bulletin board. She stared at the board. She lifted a hand, rested it on the board.

Will stopped then and looked back to Alice. He rested a hand on Ellinor's arm.

"Uh, oh," said Will. "I think Auntie is weirding out on us, Sis."

Further down the hall, Miles slowed and turned about, appearing to sense something. Anna and Jack stopped beside him. They watched Will and Ellinor move up beside Alice.

"Alice?" asked Ellinor. "What is it?"

Alice lightly brushed her hand across the bulletin board. There was a thin glow beneath her fingertips. She spoke as if from somewhere very far away.

"Chalk…" a slight tilt of her head. "Bubble gum."

Will's expression and tone was now cool and serious.

"Alice? Alice, where are you?"

"One plus two is three. Three plus four is seven." She tilts her head sharply now while keeping her focus on the bulletin board. "Red ball… red ball…"

"Right…"

"Atomic weight…" Alice furrowed her brow. "My mother told me to choose the very best one and you are it." Her expression turned dark, her tone somber. "Stop… drop… cover."

"Alice?"

Alice's expression changed again… surprised.

"Oh! Bologna sandwich…"

She grew quiet. Again. Will and Ellinor waited. Miles stepped toward them, leaving Anna and Jack watching. Alice turned to the group; her expression transitioned slowly from somewhere far away to now numbly overcome.

"Not empty. Real. Real. Alive."

"Excuse me?" asked Ellinor.

"Teachers. Students. Classrooms, hallways… Laughing, learning… noise." Alice appeared dazed. "But… the same… every day; The same. Always… every day… the same. The same day."

She delicately brushed her cheek with her fingertips. "Over and over and over."

"Uh, yeah…" said Will. "How do you—"

Alice's thoughts continued to drift. "All the lines. All the lines come together. Here. Intersection. Crossroads… It's all… here."

Ellinor reached out and took Alice's hand. "Alice?"

"Today," said Alice.

"What happened today?" asked Ellinor. "What about today? Why is today different?"

Miles took another step nearer the others. His words were calm and matter-of-fact.

"It's ending," he stated.

Alice slowly turned her head, looked to Miles, through Miles.

"It is… ending." She brushed at her cheek again. "It is time to go home."

Chapter Five

Miles was sitting at his desk, hovering over paperwork. A philanthropic wind farm project involved lots and lots of paperwork.

Alice was at her place before the window, looking out at the bright, clear day. She closed her eyes to the sunshine that was streaming in, warming her face. She lifted a hand, slowly, palm out to the sun. Her breasts rose and fell, slow, regular.

Young Jack was sitting on the floor in the middle of the room. He was building a castle with children's blocks. The structure was very well done. There also appeared to be some magic involved. There was a tiny gray cloud hovering above the structure, and a moat encircled the castle. In the moat, live miniature alligators.

Will and Ellinor came into the study. Miles looked up briefly, returned to his paperwork. Alice turned briefly from the window, returned to the view outside. Her raised hand turned slightly. There was the hint of tiny sparks dancing from fingertip to fingertip. She closed her eyes again. A faint glow enveloped her hand, lay across her face.

"Mrs. Bailey has lunch about ready," said Ellinor.

"Be there in a minute," said Miles, without looking up from his work.

Will moved over to Jack. He took a moment to look at the castle of children's blocks, then squatted down beside the boy.

"Cool castle."

"Thank you." Jack positioned another block on the structure.

"Looks like you've done this before." Will shifted position as he tried to get comfortable on the floor.

"Some." Jack shrugged.

"At school?"

"Some."

"Right," said Will. "You liked it there? At school?"

Jack shrugged again, said nothing. He continued building his castle. The tiny clouds above the castle darkened. There was a flash of light within the clouds.

"I'm going to miss my friends," said Jack then, unexpectedly.

"Right," Will said again. "Sure."

One of the alligators in the moat surfaced, glided forward and slid again beneath the surface.

"What are your plans now, Jack?" asked Will. "What would you like to do?"

Jack stopped with a block in hand, thinking about the question. Ellinor listened, watched from several steps behind Will.

"I have to take care of Grandma." Jack placed the block into position.

"Right," said Jack. "That's important. Your grandma is a great lady."

"Yes. She is."

"You and your grandma, you've been together a long time."

Jack hesitated again. He looked now directly at Will, for the first time.

"Tomorrow's my birthday," he said. "I'm going to be seven."

This took Will a bit by surprise. The statement brought home the reality of the boy's situation. Jack had been six years old for half a century. And it was only now that they were out of Sharp Park that time had begun to move forward again for Jack and his grandmother.

"Umm, right," said Will. "Well… we should do something about that."

§

The front door opened and Will came into the foyer. He absently closed the door behind him, sorted through the mail as he started across the room.

Sensing something, he looked up, stopped.

Mr. Gray was standing in the middle of the room, looking coolly at Will. Will hesitated, smiled, and held the mail out to Mr. Gray.

"Good morning, Mr. Gray."

"Good morning, William." Mr. Gray took the mail. "Thank you."

"My pleasure." He gave Mr. Gray a thoughtful curl of the brow. "Say… Mr. Gray. Your thoughts on birthday cake. Chocolate or white?"

Mr. Gray had been dealing with unexpected questions from Will for the young man's entire life.

"White cake, chocolate frosting," he answered with hardly a moment's hesitation.

"Sounds good. I like it," said Will. He started away in the direction of the kitchen. "Thank you, Mr. Gray."

Anna stood at the water's edge. The ever-present fog drifted slowly past. The only sound was that of the light surf.

Miles walked up the beach toward her. As he neared, he spoke nostalgically.

"Do you remember the first time we came here?"

"The six of us." Anna kept her gaze to the horizon. "The motel had been open only a few weeks."

"The fog was the same." Miles stood beside Anna, looked out toward the same horizon in the distance. "I don't remember the smell being this bad."

"It was. You were too busy to notice."

"Ah, youth," said Miles nostalgically.

"Absolutely," said Anna. She looked from the ocean to Miles. Her attention drifted then to the embankment up the beach, the unseen motel on the other side. "Jack was three when Jason and Sarah came here one summer. The boy loved it. He talked of nothing else for weeks afterward."

"And so when…"

"Yes. We came here. Jack brought *here* to us."

They stood silent then, listening to the surf. After a few moments, Miles turned his head and looked up the beach. A lone figure waited in the distance.

Jason stood patiently waiting. He looked old and withered.

Miles turned to Anna. He raised a questioning brow.

Anna gave a kind smile and gentle nod in reply. Miles placed a soft hand on

Anna's arm before starting away. He walked up the beach toward Jason.

Jason started forward and they met a dozen paces from Anna.

"Thank you, Clive," he said.

"We have only a few minutes," said Miles. "Try to make the best of them."

"Thank you." Jason continued up the beach toward Anna, stopped two paces from her. He waited, watched for some sign.

Anna turned her attention back to the sea, to the horizon beyond.

"Mother," said Jason.

"Hello, Jason," said Anna, not yet looking at him.

Further up the beach, Miles reached the base of the embankment. He turned about, stuffed his hands into his jacket pockets and watched Anna and Jason for several moments.

He started then up the side of the embankment.

§

Alice stood before the window in her room, the sunlight warming her, feeding her. The world was quiet, calm, peaceful. Her eyes were closed, and she drifted, drifted…

A dark place, an empty place. A void. There, in the distance, a shifting shadow in the black. It reached out to her, reached for her…

She opened her eyes, wide, afraid. She quickly sucked in a breath and leaned forward, placed both hands flat on the glass of the window. She spoke in a desperate, fearful, harsh whisper.

"It wasn't him. Not, not him. Dark, dark, so dark…"

She pulled back from the window, stepped back, stumbled back. She turned about, looked into the room, ready to call out, to warn them, to warn everyone.

But she was alone.
"It's coming," she said. "It's coming."

~ end of pilot episode

Episode One: "Last Day at Sharp Park"
Series: "Miles Bennett"